This book belongs to:

....

FOR MY THREE 'MANE' GIRLS – RACHEL, PAM AND SIDNIE

EGMONT

We bring stories to life

First published in 2013 in the United States by Little, Brown and Company
This edition published in 2019 by Egmont UK Limited The Yellow Building,
1 Nicholas Road, London W11 4AN

www.egmont.co.uk

Licensed by:

www.mylittlepony.com

HASBRO and its logo, MY LITTLE PONY and all related characters
are trademarks of Hasbro and are used with permission.
©2019 Hasbro. All rights reserved.

978 1 4052 9498 0

70530/001

Printed and bound in Great Britain by CPI Group

MIX
Paper from
responsible sources
FSC® C020471

Twilight Sparkle
and the Spell

WRITTEN BY G. M. BERROW

Contents

CHAPTER 1
A Crown Achievement

All of Equestria had been celebrating since the joyous wedding of Shining Armor and Princess Mi Amore Cadenza – or Cadance, as she was called. The citizens of Equestria, including the newly recovered Crystal Empire, were living in a time of happiness and prosperity. Apples grew in the orchards, creatures big and small played in the lush green fields, and ponies of all three tribes lived in harmony. And now, another promising young royal had joined the highest ranks of pony society. It seemed like the cherry on top of a delicious ice-cream sundae.

Ponies of all kinds from the far reaches of Princess Celestia's kingdom were curious about the new princess who had just been crowned. She was a young Unicorn pony with a violet-hued hide, a beautiful purple-and-pink striped mane, and incredible abilities. Her name was Twilight Sparkle, and she was indeed very special. Stories of her amazing magical gifts had travelled all the way from San Franciscolt to Manehattan. These tales had started to become legendary – especially the one about the time she defeated the evil Queen Chrysalis in order to save the royal court of Canterlot. All the ponies in Equestria were excited to see what wonders Twilight Sparkle's reign would bring.

Twilight was excited too. Not only did she bear an esteemed new title, but she had received her very own set of wings. *Real* Pegasus wings! She was officially part of a special breed of pony called an Alicorn. This meant that Twilight was now able to harness the magical powers of the Unicorns, the flight abilities of the Pegasi, and the strength of a good, true heart of an Earth Pony. She was becoming more like her teacher, the talented and kind Princess Celestia, every day.

Although it was very exciting for Twilight to become an Alicorn, she didn't take her new gifts for granted. It was an honour to be part of something so rare. She didn't care about all the shiny jewels and castle rooms she'd been given. She was happy to remain in Ponyville for now. She loved to spend time in her library with Spike, the baby dragon who was her number-one assistant, and having barrels of fun with her best friends.

Ever since Princess Celestia had sent Twilight away from Canterlot to study and learn the magic of friendship, she had felt that Ponyville was her true home. Twilight was uncertain how she would feel if she had to leave – let alone rule a kingdom.

It was true that Twilight Sparkle loved to help other ponies, to teach them the interesting facts she'd read about in the pages of her beloved books. She also enjoyed her position as leader of the Ponyville Winter Wrap-Up. But being in charge of a kingdom of ponies didn't seem easy. Twilight was nervous. She still had so much to learn. But, then again, there was *always* more to learn. The world was so vast and fascinating!

One afternoon in Ponyville, just after the Pegasi had moved some clouds into the sky for a short rainfall, Twilight went home to scour every book in her library yet again. She was hoping for some guidance on exactly how a pony could become a great princess and leader.

There was bound to be some information in one of her books that could help her. She thought she was on to something when she first laid a hoof on the pages of *The Princess Bridle*. It was one of her favourite stories about royal ponies, but not quite right.

'What about this one, Twi?' Spike said, pulling a dusty book from one of the low shelves. He couldn't reach the higher ones without a ladder. The book was titled *Purple Reign* by Crystal Ball. But that was no good either. It just had lots of song lyrics in it.

'Spike!' Twilight exclaimed. 'What am I going to do?' She threw her hoof up into the air. 'I need some help. I just know there's more to being a leader than what I already know.' Twilight began to pace the room in her usual manner. She did this so often that the floorboards had worn down, forming a large circle. Spike liked to call it the Twilight Zone.

Spike furrowed his scaly brow and clapped his claws together. 'That's it!' He sprang up and knocked several titles from the shelf. A moment later, he appeared in the pile of fallen books, clutching one with a familiar blue-and-yellow cover. Twilight recognised it immediately as *Daring Do and the Trek to the Terrifying Tower*. She had already read all the books in the series about the fearless pony adventurer at least three times.

Twilight cocked her head to the side. 'I don't get it, Spike. What's Daring Do got to 'do' with it?'

'Well, you know how Daring has to rescue a pony who's been locked in a tower surrounded by a moat filled with sharp-toothed piranhas?'

'Yeah . . . so?'

'And you know how she has to dive into the water to reach the tower, even though fish are secretly her biggest fear?'

'Spike! Spit it out!' Twilight exclaimed. 'Do you have an idea of how to help me or not?' She was beginning to look a bit stressed. Her mane had gone frizzy and one of her eyes was twitching ever so slightly. Twilight took her responsibilities very seriously – sometimes too seriously.

'Well, basically Daring Do wants to overcome her fears once and for all. So she asks some older ex-adventurer ponies, like Professor A. B. Ravenhoof, for tips on how to do it!' Spike spread his short arms wide in triumph.

Aha! It was so obvious to Twilight now.
She needed guidance from someone
wiser. 'Why didn't *I* think of that?'
Twilight's face lit up, thinking of all the
ponies she could interview. 'Good work,
Spike! It's perfect.' Spike blushed.
He loved nothing more than to be a
good assistant to his best friend. But
he could hardly say 'You're welcome!'
before Twilight Sparkle was out of
the door to find out about the great
leaders of Equestria – straight from the
horses' mouths.

CHAPTER 2
A Foal House

'Who in Ponyville might be able to help me?' Twilight said aloud as she trotted through the town square. She caught sight of Mayor Mare walking on the opposite side of the courtyard, heading into the town hall with a group of important-looking ponies. The mayor ran

their whole town! She would definitely
know a thing or two about leadership.
It was a good place to start.

But by the time she reached the steps
of the town hall, the mayor was already
behind closed doors. 'Sorry, Princess
Twilight,' Senior Mint, the tall green
guard pony said. 'Ms Mayor Mare is in
a long meeting about next year's Summer
Sun Celebration.'

Twilight slumped in defeat. 'Oh well.
But you don't have to call me Princess.
Just Twilight will do.' Senior Mint
nodded, embarrassed.

'Will you tell her I stopped by?'
Twilight asked. Maybe they could
talk later.

'Yes, of course, Princess Twilight.' He
cupped a hoof over his mouth. 'Oops, I
mean *Just Twilight*.'

'Thanks!' She flashed her shiny white smile, turned on her hoof, and headed back to the town square. Suddenly, she smelt the scent of something sweet and scrumptious. Her tummy rumbled.

'Fresh cupcakes! Extra icing!' shouted Carrot Cake, the town baker. He was pulling a pink-and-yellow cart filled with sugary delicacies of every flavour and colour. Maybe it was time for a snack!

'Hello, Mr Cake!' Twilight said, trotting up to the cart, which had begun to draw a crowd of hungry ponies. Twilight hadn't seen such a commotion since the last apple juice sale at Sweet Apple Acres.

'Hi there, Twilight Sparkle!' said
Mr Cake.

'Is this your new treat cart?' she asked.
'What a wonderful idea!'

'Mrs Cake and I are always trying to
come up with new ways to share our
desserts with the ponies of Ponyville.'
Pumpkin Cake and Pound Cake, twin
foals, giggled and trotted alongside their
father. Pound Cake, who was a Pegasus,
beat his little wings until he was hovering
near a tray of pink and purple pastries.
When his father wasn't watching, he
sneakily snatched one and ate it in
a single greedy bite. His
sister, Pumpkin Cake,
jumped as high as she
could to grab one, but
she couldn't quite
reach. She finally used

her Unicorn magic to steal a blue
cupcake and deliver it gently to her
mouth. She licked her lips. Then
she burped.

'Plus, the babies love to get out of the
shop,' Mr Cake continued, too busy to
notice his little foals' naughty actions.
'Fresh air does them good!'

Twilight watched as Pumpkin and
Pound chased each other in circles and
through the legs of a nearby grey Pegasus
pony. The pony wobbled helplessly before
toppling over into a nearby rosebush.
When she popped her head out, her
lemon-yellow mane was adorned with
prickly thorns. 'Mr Cake! Do you have
any muffins today?' she called. Her hoof
got caught on a branch, and she tumbled
onto the soft grass.

'Fresh out of muffins, unfortunately,'

Carrot replied, looking concerned.

'Well, *I'll* take one cupcake, please.' Twilight licked her lips. Mr Cake reached inside the glass display case, but all that was left were crumbs. 'Oh dear, we seem to be out of *everything*!' He frowned.

'Why don't you trot back to SugarCube Corner with us?' Carrot offered. 'Mrs Cake is sure to have whipped up some more by now.'

Twilight hesitated. She was supposed to be on a fact-finding mission, not eating cakes. Her stomach rumbled again and Pumpkin Cake giggled.

'I guess that's my answer,' Twilight said. 'Just for a few minutes, though. Then I have to get back to my quest.'

The twins cheered and hopped on Twilight's back for a ride to the bakery. 'Giddyup!' they chorused.

'Mrs Cake, this rainbow chip…*mmmf*…
delight is…delicious,' Twilight said with a
full mouth. A dollop of pink icing made
its way down her chin. 'Excuse me,' she
said as she cleaned her face. 'I don't
mean to eat and run like this, but I really
must go.'

'Of course, Princess,' Mrs Cake said,
bowing quickly. She continued to pipe
a tube of icing onto a strawberry-layer
cake, creating a beautiful border of
plump roses.

Twilight blushed. 'You really don't
have to call me that,' she replied. This
princess business was tricky. Maybe she
should put up a banner in the town
square telling everyone to treat her as

they normally would. 'I'm just the same old Twilight, really.'

She caught sight of her reflection in the shiny cake display case. Other than the new wings, she still looked the same. She wasn't even wearing her tiara. 'In fact, I don't really know how to be a princess at all. That's what I'm doing today. I'm trying to ask some older ponies what it means to be a leader, but I don't want to ask Princess Celestia – that would be embarrassing – and when I tried to see Mayor Mare, she was busy and...' Everything spilled out at once.

Mrs Cake furrowed her brow in motherly concern. 'My goodness, that sounds like a sticky situation. Why don't you visit your big brother and Princess Cadance?'

Twilight smiled. What a great idea!

Her BBBFF (Big Brother Best Friend Forever) Shining Armor and new Pegasister-in-law had much more royal experience than she did. 'You're a genius! They are bound to have some royal advice!'

Carrot Cake popped his head in from the storeroom. 'We're not out of royal icing! We have a whole carriage full back here, my dear!'

'No, Carrot,' Mrs Cake shouted back. 'Royal *advice*. For Twilight!'

She shook her head, sighing. 'Stallions. They never listen.'

Twilight chuckled as she made her way out of the door. 'Maybe I'd better talk to Cadance and *not* Shining Armor.' She was feeling more confident now that she had a real plan. 'Thanks for the terrific tips and treats, Mrs Cake! Bye, Pumpkin! Bye, Pound!' And then the young monarch was off to find out exactly what made a royal pony tick.

CHAPTER 3
Empire State of Mind

Twilight Sparkle didn't think it was possible, but the Crystal Empire looked even more beautiful than the last time she'd been there. The winding, cobble-gem streets and tall spires sparkled in the sunshine. It had been a long journey, but it was well worth it to be back.

Everything appeared to be fully restored to its former glory, partly thanks to her, of course, though she would never brag about it. The Crystal Empire had been through many dark days after the evil King Sombra tried to keep the source of the Empire's power – the Crystal Heart – hidden away. The Crystal Heart, charged by the power of the ponies' love, was the only object that was able to offer the Empire protection. Once it was stolen, the kingdom was overtaken by darkness.

Luckily, Princess Celestia had put Twilight to the test when she recruited her and her friends to help. They came to the rescue, putting on the long-forgotten Crystal Faire while Twilight searched for the Crystal Heart. When Twilight finally succeeded in recovering the precious, magical gemstone, not only did she pass her test, but balance was also restored to the city.

As Twilight walked past a group of Crystal ponies, she smiled and waved. 'Good afternoon, everyone!'

'Hey, Princess Twilight Sparkle!' they shouted in response. 'Welcome back!'

A sparkling teal-coloured pony with a light blue mane jumped up and down in excitement. The pony was named Glitter Dance and reminded Twilight of her eternally energetic friend, Pinkie Pie. 'We're going to the Crystal Lake today!' she exclaimed. 'Come and play with us!'

Twilight politely declined but was pleased with the invitation. The ponies were having tons of fun with one another, which was always a good sign. Every corner of the kingdom appeared to be filled with light and love. It was certainly the perfect place for Shining Armor and Princess Cadance to live and rule.

'Twily!' a handsome white stallion with a blue mane yelled from across the courtyard. Shining Armor hadn't seen his sister since her coronation. He galloped over and embraced her in a classic big-brother hug. 'How's my second-favourite princess?' He knocked her cheek lovingly with his hoof.

'Hey, now!' Twilight laughed. 'I was around first!'

'Only kidding!' he said as Princess Cadance trotted over to join them.

'You're *both* my favourite princesses.'

'Cadance!' Twilight called out.
'*Sunshine…sunshine…*' she started, looking to the elegant princess for acknowledegment.

'*Ladybirds awake!*' Cadance yelled in joyous response.

The two of them sang in unison as they hopped around and shook their tails at each other. '*Clap your hooves and do a little shake!*' It had been their secret tailshake since Twilight was just a little filly and Cadance was her foal-sitter. It was still amusing after all these years, even though a couple of nearby ponies watched the scene in confusion. It was unusual to see their princess acting so silly.

'So what brings you to the Crystal Empire, little sis?' Shining Armor asked.

'Isn't royal life great?' He beamed with pride and smiled wide. His little sister had come so far in her studies that she'd achieved princess status.

'Well...that's sort of why I'm here.' Twilight dropped her eyes to the ground and scuffed a hoof around. 'I don't know how to act! I don't feel anything like a princess, and it's weird to have everyone call me that. I don't feel very graceful... Not like you, Cadance.'

'Oh, Twilight!' said Shining Armor. 'It isn't easy. But you're doing great!'

Twilight knew he was trying to help, but she couldn't resist rolling her eyes a little bit. 'Of course you would say that. You're my brother – you have to think so!'

'Chill out, Twily. Being royalty is easy! Right, Cadance?'

Cadance's face became serious. 'No,

Shining Armor. It's not as simple as that. I completely understand what she's going through.' She turned to her fellow princess. 'Maybe I can help you, Twilight.'

She started by leading Twilight Sparkle down the street and through the city. Twilight was happy to follow.

CHAPTER 4
A Tail to Tell

It was a busy day in the Crystal Empire. The streets were bustling with Crystal ponies rushing home from the markets and shops, their packs filled with fresh apples and other luxuries.

'Good afternoon, Moondust!' Cadance greeted an iridescent white pony with a sleek silver mane. She was selling baskets of Crystal berries at a little stand near the fountain. 'How are your foals?'

The pony beamed as she bowed to the two princesses. 'They are wonderful! Would you like some fresh Crystal berries?' Moondust asked, and gave them each a small bunch. The sweet tartness exploded in Twilight's mouth as she devoured them. Twilight made a mental note to bring some back for the Cakes. The berries would taste delicious in a pie.

'Thank you very much!' Twilight said as they walked away. How did Cadance do that – remember the names of a whole kingdom's residents? Twilight sometimes found it difficult to remember the names of just the entire Apple family.

'I always try to remember every pony in the kingdom, because each one is special,' Cadance explained as they walked. 'We all play our part in making the kingdom a happy and fun place to live.'

Twilight sighed. Cadance definitely had a point, but all these new responsibilities were starting to add up.

'You're such a great princess, Cadance,' Twilight said. 'I wish I could be like you. I feel so lost.'

'I didn't always feel so confident,' Cadance said.

'You didn't?' Twilight asked, trying to think of a time when Cadance had seemed as lost as she felt now.

'When I was found as a baby Pegasus, in a forest far, far away...' Cadance began the familiar tale. Twilight listened intently as Cadance recounted her path to becoming the great pony leader she was today.

Cadance told her how
some Earth Ponies
from a nearby
village took
her in as
their own
little filly.
And as she

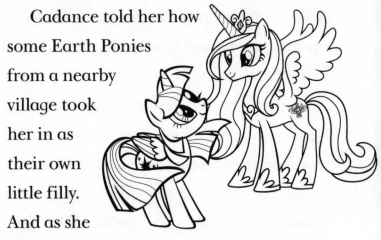

grew up, the natural love and compassion
she had for others filled everyone with
warmth and the urge to protect her.

But all was not well for long.

An evil pony enchantress named
Prismia lived alone nearby. She rarely
came out of her cottage because she felt
nothing but jealousy for the other ponies
in the village – the way they loved and
took care of one another. And yet, she
had no one who cared for her. Prismia

wore a powerful necklace, which she cared for more than anything else in the world, and it served to amplify the evil and jealousy within her own heart. When Prismia's bad feelings and the power of the necklace finally overtook her, she cast a spell on the villagers that leeched all the love from their homes. She hoped to capture some of that love for herself.

Cadance decided that she couldn't let that happen, so she went to see Prismia. Luckily, the enchantress's powerful necklace also amplified the power of Cadance's love, and she soon defeated Prismia with her incredible kindness. Once Prismia changed her horrible ways, Cadance was surrounded by magical energy and transported to a strange place – a place that no one except Princess Celestia had ever been! So when Celestia discovered Cadance in that mysterious location, her fate was sealed. The princess brought her back to Canterlot to raise her as her very own royal niece – the special young Princess Cadance.

Princess Cadance's talent had always been her ability to spread love wherever she went – settling conflicts and bringing ponies together. In her final exam at Celestia's school of magic, Cadance was even able to make two known rival pony families of Canterlot become best friends for life.

'So I spent a long time in Canterlot just resolving conflicts and helping other ponies find love. I never really experienced it for myself.' Cadance giggled. 'Even though I *did* have a crush on your brother.'

Twilight made a disgusted face. 'Yuck.'

'Everyone was telling me what a great princess I would be someday, but I just didn't feel like I knew what to do!' Cadance said. Twilight nodded in enthusiastic agreement. Now they were talking. 'So I went to Princess Celestia for advice.'

'And…?' Twilight asked, all ears.

'She asked me if I *felt* like a true leader.' Cadance turned to her young companion. 'I told her that no, sadly, I didn't.'

'And…?' Twilight repeated. She could hardly take the suspense!

Cadance continued, 'She told me about an ancient spell that had the power to make anyone who was destined to lead become the pony they were meant to be.'

Twilight smiled. She *knew* that there was an answer to all of this – and of course it was a spell!

True leadership was only an
enchantment away.

The two ponies soon
found themselves
standing in front of a giant crystal statue
of Cadance. The sun shone through it,
creating hundreds of tiny rainbows in
the water flowing through the fountain.
'Wow, they must really love you here,
Cadance.' Twilight could never imagine
having a statue of herself. It was a
bit much.

Cadance shook her head and
shrugged. 'Oh, I guess so!' she said,
chuckling.

The famous, powerful Crystal Heart

stood next to the statue, shining brilliantly with the magic of the Crystal ponies. Thankfully, it was safely displayed right where Twilight had last left it, rather than hidden away with some evil king. Rescuing the heart once had been difficult enough. She didn't want to have to do it again.

'So where can I find this leader spell, then? Can you teach it to me? Is it in one of the old spell books?' Twilight asked eagerly. As soon as she learned the words from Cadance, she'd be on her way back to Ponyville. Then everything would be solved.

'Oh, no, Twilight.' Cadance shook her head. 'This spell isn't something that can just be learned. The Crystal Heart Spell can only be revealed when a future leader of Equestria understands what her biggest

* ✩ * 35 * ✩ *

challenge in leadership will be. Only then will she know how to rule, in her heart.'

Twilight furrowed her brow in confusion. What in Equestria was Cadance talking about? *Revealed?* Twilight was somehow supposed to get some random spell to appear out of thin air? This was going to be trickier than she'd expected.

'How am I supposed to do that?!'

'I can help you with one clue, just as Celestia did with me.' Cadance's voice was gentle and reassuring. 'Just think about the elements that make up a great kingdom, Twilight.'

'The Elements of Harmony?' Twilight asked. It was the first thing that popped into her mind, so it was probably too obvious.

'Not exactly...' Cadance said. 'What

are the best things we have in Equestria?'

Twilight looked completely baffled. Cadance thought it might be time for a different approach. So she began to recount her search for the spell in greater depth. Cadance warned Twilight, though, that the spell worked differently for every pony. It couldn't be repeated.

'Once I received the clue myself, I decided to start by asking my friends what they thought,' Cadance remembered. 'They had all sorts of crazy ideas about what they liked in a kingdom.'

'Like what?'

'Well, my friend Buttercream said she thought every kingdom should have a chocolate fountain in the centre. And another pony I knew, Sky Chariot, suggested a curfew time for all ponies to be home by.' Cadance scrunched up her face in distaste. 'I didn't really agree with any of them, but I used their ideas anyway.'

Twilight nodded along as she listened to the story.

'But nothing happened!' Cadance said dramatically. 'The spell was nowhere to be found, and I was more lost than ever.'

Twilight's eyes grew wide. 'So how did you find it?'

'One day, I was sitting by the lake just outside Canterlot,' Cadance recalled. 'I thought about how all I had ever done was listen to the suggestions or commands of other ponies.'

'Like the way they would always ask you to help them fall in love?' Twilight asked.

'Yes, exactly! I never made any

decisions for myself.' Cadance stared out into the water of the crystal fountain. 'As soon as I realised this, the spell appeared, shimmering in gold letters on the surface of the lake.'

'Wow...' Twilight cooed, imagining the pretty scene.

'As I read the spell aloud, I instantly knew that my destiny was to lead other ponies with my strengths of True Love and Tolerance. But the only way to do it was by listening to my *own* heart as well.'

CHAPTER 5
A Gift Horse

Cadance led Twilight through a wooden door and into a castle bedroom. It was decked out in rich, royal velvets of deep purple and gold. Precious gems of every colour adorned the bed frame and hung from the chandelier. The early evening light shining through tall windows onto the lavish furnishings was dazzling.

Twilight blinked in disbelief. 'This room is all mine?'

'Well, not *all* yours!' Spike popped out from behind the purple curtains and did a dance. 'Surprise!' Cadance laughed at the little dragon's antics.

'Spike!' Twilight instantly felt guilty for leaving him behind. 'Sorry I left Ponyville in such a rush.'

'It's just lucky you came back here when you did,' said Spike. 'I almost ate that bed while I was waiting.' Spike's eyes grew large as he looked around. Jewels and crystals were his favourite meal. It had taken a lot of self-control to keep him from nibbling the furniture.

'Good thing you didn't.' Twilight's eyes

landed on a small, wrapped golden box that was sitting on the bed. 'Spike, you didn't have to bring me a present. It's not my birthday!'

'But I didn't...' said Spike.

'It's from me,' explained Cadance, nudging it towards Twilight with her muzzle. 'Just a little gift from one princess to another.'

Twilight tore open the packaging. Inside was a beautiful necklace made of purple jewels. At the centre was a large gem in the shape of a heart. It had a quality to it that Twilight had seen only one other place...

'Cadance, is this your favourite necklace? From when we were growing up?' As a filly, Twilight had admired the necklace. It had always seemed to be extra special in some way that she couldn't quite put her hoof on.

Cadance smiled warmly. 'Of course it is! I think it's time that a new princess wore it proudly.'

'Oh, Cadance!' Twilight put the necklace on and spun around. 'I'll take such good care of it! Thank you.'

'Of course, my dear new sister,' Cadance said as she made her way to the door. 'I just want you to know one thing.'

Twilight was spinning around in front of the mirror, dreamy-eyed. 'Yes?' she said.

'The rare gem in the middle has been enchanted with a powerful charm,' Cadance explained. 'As long as the pony wearing it is filled with the magic of love and positivity, the necklace will wrap her in warmth and protection.'

'It sounds amazing!' Twilight said.

'Wait, is this the same necklace from the story? That Prismia wore?'

'It very well may be,' said Cadance with a wink before she turned serious again. 'But you must also remember that if the pony wearing it does *not* display love and positivity, it will only magnify her negative thoughts! Be careful, Twilight. If you stay true to your heart, the spell will soon reveal itself.' And with that, Cadance was gone.

'Got it,' Twilight replied lazily, exhaustion from the long journey finally overtaking her. She climbed into the comfy bed and nuzzled down under the covers. In the morning, she would begin to look for the elements of a perfect kingdom. 'True to your heart...' she whispered before falling into a sweet, dreamless slumber.

She'd only been there a day, but Twilight
Sparkle's Crystal Suite was already a
mess. All the books from the shelf in the
room were pulled out, littering the floor
and bed. Some were open at pages filled
with spells and history lessons; others lay
closed in stacks. Spike sat on the window
seat, gazing out at the panoramic view
of the Crystal Empire and then looking
closer with a telescope. He was trying
to guess how many crystals were out
there and also how yummy each one
would taste.

'Where did Cadance say she started
looking for the spell?' Twilight asked
Spike, who hopped down and started
restacking the books.

'I don't know!' Spike replied. 'I was up here waiting for you, remember? I didn't hear her story.'

Twilight picked up the box that held her gorgeous new necklace. As soon as she slipped it on and looked in the mirror, she knew exactly what to do. 'She asked her friends for their opinions – that's what Cadance did!' Twilight exclaimed. 'Spike, take down a letter! No – make that *five* letters! I'm going to hold a secret spell summit with my best friends.'

A meeting of the greatest minds in Ponyville was just what was needed.

CHAPTER 6
On a Scroll

Spike had been busy all day delivering the
invitations for Twilight's emergency secret
meeting. He'd visited Fluttershy's cottage
first. She accepted and asked Spike if he
wanted to come inside and play with her
new fruit bat, Toby. 'He's so shy, and I
think he could use a friend like you,

Spike,' she said in her gentle voice.

'Sorry, Fluttershy! I have all these scrolls to deliver. Maybe Toby and I can "hang out" later!' Spike chuckled at his own joke, but Fluttershy looked confused. 'Get it? "Hang out?" Because bats hang upside down?'

'Oh yes! See you at the meeting!'

Next, he found Applejack working in the orchard at Sweet Apple Acres. She

bucked her hind legs against a tree and a batch of juicy apples came tumbling down into a basket. 'A meeting with Twilight?' Applejack looked relieved. 'Phew! I haven't seen her for days! I was about to send out the Apple family search party.'

'Did someone say *party*?!' An excited Pinkie Pie popped out from behind a tree. 'Because my Party Watch just went off!' She held up her hoof to show Spike and Applejack a bright neon accessory. It looked like a watch, but instead of numbers it just had pictures of colourful balloons, streamers and confetti with the word *party* spelled out twelve times. Little blinking lights rimmed the edge, and a honking noise was being emitted from a tiny speaker at the top.

'But where are all the numbers?'

Applejack asked, confused.

'Who needs numbers?' Pinkie shrugged.

'To see what time it is, silly!' Applejack threw her hooves in the air.

'But it does tell the time! It's party time...all the time!' Pinkie shouted with glee. 'Now who said the magic word, huh? Huh?!' She came up to Spike and looked him straight in the eye. 'Was it you?'

'It's not a party, really...but here you go, Pinkie.' Spike handed her a scroll.

She unfurled it and read the message. 'A secret meeting party?! Oh goody! I have to go and get ready!' And Pinkie Pie bounced off towards her house.

'Thanks, Spike,' Applejack said, shaking her head. 'I guess you can count me and Pinkie in.'

Rarity, on the other hand, was less thrilled about the invitation. She peered down at the scroll through her purple cat's-eye work glasses. 'I'm in the middle of making a huge order of hornaments! Can this wait until later?' Rarity was always trying to finish some new garment or accessory for her Carousel Boutique.

'Twilight said it was an emergency.' Spike looked down at his feet. He didn't want to upset Rarity, because he really liked her. But she always responded to a few well-worded compliments.

'Say, Rarity... have you done something special to your mane? It looks super-duper shiny!'

'Well, I did go to the spa this morning to have my hooves done and they used some new conditioner…' Rarity began. Five minutes later, Spike was still standing there. '…and so I said, 'Darling, if you must do my tail as well, just do it.' I knew it would be worth it!'

'Well, it looks great! Gotta run!' Spike quickly said before heading off down the road. He had spent a while listening to chatter about the latest beauty treatments in Ponyville, and now he was running late. Luckily, he had only one stop left. Rainbow Dash was the last pony he had to invite to Twilight's secret meeting.

'Special delivery for one Miss Rainbow Dash!' Spike shouted half-heartedly at the clouds. He was ready to call it a day by the time he reached Ponyville Park. It was directly under Cloudsdale, so there was a

good chance of finding the Pegasus there.

'Rainbow Daaaash!' he called out impatiently. 'I have a very important invitation to a very secret meeting at Twilight Sparkle's cottage!'

'Hold your ponies, Spike,' Rainbow Dash said, swooping down from a cloud. 'I'm comin'!'

Rainbow zoomed by a cloud that looked empty, but hidden inside was nosy Gilda the Griffon – and she had heard every word!

Suddenly, the 'secret meeting' was not so secret.

✸ ✸ ✸

'So what is this all about, Twi?' Applejack asked as she bit into one of the apple fritters she'd brought for the meeting. All five of Twilight's best friends had turned up, even though they had other things to do. Twilight knew she was lucky that they'd come to help her, no questions asked. It filled Twilight with a sense of pride that made her new necklace shine doubly bright.

Twilight cleared her throat and looked at each of the ponies in the circle. 'Thank you all for coming—' she began, and was immediately interrupted by Rarity.

'Is that divine necklace around your neck made of Cosmic Spectrum?' She stared at Twilight's new accessory with desire. 'I have only seen pictures of it in books! My, it's gorgeous! It almost looks like a mini version of the Crystal Heart.'

Rarity trotted over to get a closer look.

'Thanks! It was a present from Princess Cadance.'

'You know what they say about Cosmic Spectrum...' Rarity added, turning to the other ponies. 'When you wear it, you must remember—'

'Oh, totally. Yeah, I know all about it,' Twilight said in order to keep the meeting moving. She didn't want to listen to Rarity talk about gemstones right now. The clock was ticking! Rarity shrugged, a little hurt. She trotted back to her spot and plopped down.

'*Anyway*, thank you all for coming at such short notice.' Twilight looked around at each of her friends with genuine gratitude. 'I've asked you here because I desperately need your help—'

'Ooooh! I know!' Pinkie Pie

interrupted with a squeal. 'You're planning an undercover jewel-heist mission and you want us all to join 'Sparkle's Six'?'

Twilight shook her head. 'Not exactly.'

Pinkie Pie was wearing a tan trench coat and a fedora hat in an attempt to disguise herself for the meeting. She had also brought along a drink she called 'Secret Punch' as a refreshment, but she wouldn't reveal what the ingredients were, because it was a 'super big secret'. As a result, no one wanted to drink it. 'Or... you volunteered to plan this year's Hearth's Warming Eve pageant and you need us to help?!'

'Pinkie, it's still summertime,' Rainbow Dash said, rolling her eyes.

'Whatever it is, can we just get started?' Rarity whined. 'I have lots of work to finish! Those hornaments are due in Neigh York by tomorrow morning and they aren't going to finish rhinestoning themselves.

Do you have the time, Pinkie?' Rarity motioned towards Pinkie's Party Watch.

'Sure!' Pinkie said, and looked at her wrist. 'It's 'party'.'

'Pardon me?' Rarity looked confused. Applejack and Spike couldn't help but giggle, since they knew what was coming. 'The time is party?'

'*It's party tiiiiime!*' Pinkie cheered, and did a skipping lap around the room. Everyone laughed except Rarity, who just looked annoyed.

'OK, everyone! That's enough,' Twilight said. 'Down to business.'

The ponies listened as Twilight recounted her trip to the Crystal Empire. She told them about Cadance's journey to find the Crystal Heart Spell. Twilight explained that the only way she herself would find it was with her friends' help. Just like Cadance.

'So I'll need you all to come up with some ideas. If you don't, I'll never find the spell and I'll never learn to be a leader and I'll never be a great princess!' Twilight said in one breath.

'Calm down, Twilight,' Fluttershy said, patting her on the back. 'I'm sure that we can all figure this out together.'

'Together?' Twilight asked hopefully. 'You'll help me?'

The rest of the ponies nodded and

held up their full cups of Secret Punch in a toast. 'Together!'

CHAPTER 7
Brainstorming the Castle

The six ponies had been brainstorming for ever, but Twilight felt like she was even further away from finding the spell than before. The conversation kept going in circles. They all had very different ideas about what they would do if they were in charge.

'There should be an official Cake Day!' Pinkie said, licking her lips. 'Every pony in the kingdom just eats cake all day, like a giant birthday party!'

'A royal guard made up of the fastest Pegasus ponies would be awesome,' Rainbow Dash chimed in. 'We could hold a race to find out who's the best.' She pointed to herself. 'Other than me, of course.'

Twilight took note, but knew this was not the sort of information she was looking for. She sighed. 'Applejack? Any ideas?'

Applejack's eyes lit up. 'Oooh! How about making everyone have dinner with their

families every night like the Apple family does?' she said earnestly. 'Strong families build a strong community.'

'Okaaay,' Twilight said, thinking of her own brother and parents and how far away they lived. It was a nice thought, but it wasn't practical. Not everyone was lucky enough to live near their family.

'I have an idea!' Fluttershy offered.

'You do?' Twilight replied, her ears perking up.

Fluttershy was softly spoken, but she could be very creative.

'I was just thinking how great it would be if there were a place where all the baby animals could play together in safety, far from the scary creatures of the Everfree Forest. Like a

nature reserve, but just for baby animals!
That's what I would do.'

'Ummm … OK,' Twilight said, and
wrote down the idea.

Twilight was starting to rethink her
plan. She needed real ideas about how a
kingdom works, not silly ones about baby
animals and cakes. 'Rarity, any ideas?
You've been awfully quiet over there.'

'Well, sure. If you *actually* want my
opinion …' Rarity grumbled. Ever since
she'd tried to warn Twilight about the
necklace and was shut down, Rarity
hadn't felt like saying a peep. 'I would
design a fashion line, just for the
kingdom. Exclusive pieces made from
extravagant fabrics so that every pony
would look and feel their best!'

Pinkie Pie and Fluttershy nodded in
excited agreement, but Twilight wasn't

impressed. 'Fashions, Rarity?' Twilight shook her head in defeat. 'Come on, you guys! Think outside the box!'

'Well, sorry if my idea wasn't good enough for you, *Princess*.' Rarity stuck her nose in the air. 'I wish you luck in coming up with a better one.' Then she trotted out of Twilight's cottage in a huff.

'Whoops,' Twilight said, finally realising she had hurt Rarity's feelings. 'I didn't mean to make her feel bad. I think I got a little carried away. Sorry, everyone. I guess that's enough for tonight.'

CHAPTER 8
Gilda's Got Game

Gilda the Griffon waited patiently outside Twilight's cottage until the last pony had left the secret summit. Pinkie Pie hung around for ages giving suggestions for different celebrations to throw.

'Thanks, Pinkie,' Twilight said as she walked her to the door. 'I'll certainly consider making Gummy's birthday an official holiday.' Gummy was Pinkie Pie's pet alligator.

'Great!' Pinkie squealed. 'He'll be so excited when I tell him the news!'

All of a sudden, a crazy noise started sounding from Pinkie's watch. 'I've got to go, Twilight! I totally forgot about the housewarming party at Berry Punch's new place!' With that, Pinkie bounced off into the distance.

'Finally! I thought those ponies would never leave,' Gilda said, swooping down from a cloud and landing softly in front of Twilight. 'Productive meeting, Twilight?'

'Hey! How did you know about the meeting?' Twilight asked suspiciously. It was supposed to be a secret.

'I have my ways,' Gilda said, pacing

around Twilight. 'And I listened to the whole thing. Didn't sound like your friends had *any* good ideas for your kingdom...'

'So what, Gilda?' Twilight answered back. 'You think you can do better?'

'I'm just trying to say that if *I* were a princess like you, I wouldn't be listening to anyone else's suggestions. I would do whatever I wanted! Make my kingdom all about Gilda!' The griffon cackled and flew off into the clouds again to cause some mischief elsewhere.

Twilight brushed it off. No one in their right mind would take advice from Gilda, the notorious bully. Twilight still trusted her best friends the most. And why shouldn't she? They had proved themselves to be honest and loyal.

But then again, they didn't have years

of magical study with Princess Celestia under their belts like Twilight did. And her friends had never even lived in Canterlot, so it was silly to expect them to know very much about being royal.

Twilight went back inside her cottage and looked into a large chest. It was filled with her new gowns and jewels from the coronation. None of it seemed like hers. She removed a tiara from its velvet case and placed it gently on her head. In the mirror, the sparkling white diamonds and red rubies shone brilliantly. The tiara made her stand a little taller.

Maybe Gilda had a point. Maybe the secret to leadership was listening to your own heart instead of everyone else's. Isn't that what Cadance had said?

If she was going to be a real princess, maybe she just needed to start acting like one.

The search for the Crystal Heart Spell was beginning to wear on Twilight, even though she was doing her best to try to act like a princess. She still didn't know where or how to look for it!

She even felt like she was hearing voices. For example, that morning in the Ponyville marketplace she'd asked Cheerilee which type of berries she should buy. Cheerilee had suggested the blackberries, but Twilight could've sworn she'd heard a voice coming from a stack

of crates saying, 'Who cares what *she* likes?
What kind of berries do *you* want?'

Later, when Twilight was looking after
the Cutie Mark Crusaders – Apple Bloom,
Scootaloo
and Sweetie
Belle – she'd
heard it
again.
They'd all
been in

Ponyville Park, deciding on an afternoon
activity. Twilight was getting frustrated
because she wanted to read the fillies a
story from one of her favourite books, but
all they wanted to do was play on the
swings. She was watching them when she
heard the voice again. 'Look at them!' it
whispered. 'You know what's best for
them and they didn't even listen. You're

the *princess*, for Celestia's sake!'

She'd looked around but hadn't seen anyone who could have said it.

It was so odd. Ever since Gilda the Griffon planted the idea in her head that she shouldn't listen to her friends, Twilight had started to feel that everyone else's opinions were wrong. But was Gilda right?

Twilight decided to trot through the forest in the hope of clearing her head.

She was only alone for a few moments, however, before a loud crash signalled the presence of another, familiar pink pony.

'There you are!' Pinkie Pie shouted through the trees. 'I have been looking aaaall over for you! I want to show you my

awesome plan for the new kingdom's
holiday celebrations!'

'Thanks, Pinkie. But now isn't a good
time,' Twilight said calmly. 'I'm sort
of busy.'

'OK! Will you be busy in ten minutes?'
Pinkie asked, walking
alongside her.

'Yes.' Twilight was starting to get
frustrated now. She wanted to be alone.

'OK! What about in twenty minutes?!'
Pinkie asked. To her, everything was a
game.

'No! I'm busy now, I'm busy in ten
minutes, and I'm busy in twenty minutes!'
Twilight snapped. Her necklace began to
dim, the colours churning. 'Can't you see
I don't have time to talk about your silly
little parties?'

'What?' Pinkie Pie slumped to the

ground, hurt. 'Sorry to bother you, Twilight. I was just trying to help. I'll leave you alone and go where someone wants me.'

'Finally!' Twilight sneered. 'That's the best idea you've had yet!' As she trotted off into the distance, Pinkie began to wonder what was really going on with Twilight Sparkle.

This time, she didn't think it was something a party could solve.

CHAPTER 9
A Head in the Clouds

Twilight Sparkle was planning to ask
Rainbow Dash if she'd seen Gilda the
Griffon. Even though the two of them were
no longer the best of friends, Rainbow saw
most of the comings and goings of the
residents of Ponyville. There were great
views of the town from up in the clouds.

Maybe talking to the griffon again would shed some light on the situation. There had to be more to what she tried to tell Twilight the other night after she crashed the secret meeting.

Rainbow Dash was sitting on a cloud high in the sky. She appeared to be arguing with a large group of Pegasi. She didn't hear Twilight trying to call her from below. 'Good thing I have wings now,' Twilight thought, taking off. She enjoyed the rush of cool air as she soared into the sky. It was fun to be an Alicorn!

'I have herded more clouds today than all you slowcoaches put together!' Rainbow Dash shouted at the other Pegasi.

'If you're so good, Rainbow Crash, why don't you help out the rest of us?' a big stallion named Hoops shouted back.

'Rainbow!' Twilight called out, but Rainbow didn't notice.

'You asked for it!' Rainbow shot back at Hoops, and took off into a showy barrel roll. She gathered a nearby cloud, combined it with two others, and then jumped onto it. A heavy flood of rain poured out of the bottom like a waterfall.

'Just call me Commander Hurricane!' Rainbow yelled, grinning from ear to ear.

'Rainbow Dash!' Twilight yelled a little louder. Why wasn't Rainbow listening? A princess was trying to speak to her! Twilight frowned. 'Rainbow!'

Rainbow Dash finally noticed her friend hovering there. 'Oh, hey, Twilight! Are you here to talk about my awesome plans for the new royal guard?'

'No.' Twilight rolled her eyes like answering Rainbow's question was really hard work. 'Have you seen Gilda?'

Twilight was acting really weird, and the colours on her necklace were swirling around.

'Are you OK?' Rainbow asked.

'Of course I am! Now, have you seen Gilda or not?'

'I think she's down by the farm with Trixie,' Rainbow said. 'Those two have been spending a lot of time together lately. If you ask me, it smells like trouble. Mixing pranks and magic is a bad idea, right?'

But Twilight didn't reply. She was already flying towards Sweet Apple Acres. She didn't even say 'thank you'.

CHAPTER 10
Drinking the Lily-pad Slime

A good patch of leafy foliage was always
ideal for spying. That was why Twilight
Sparkle often found herself hiding
behind trees and peering through hedges
while doing various sorts of field
research.

Today, Twilight crouched low behind a

bush near the barn at Sweet Apple Acres. She had spent the last ten minutes watching as Gilda and Trixie rolled a barrel of fresh apple juice from the stores and dumped it onto the grass. *Glug, glug, glug.* The juice spilled out quickly. Why anyone would waste it was beyond Twilight. Yet the two of them sniggered as they filled the empty barrel with gloopy green gunk that resembled the lily-pad slime from Froggy Bottom Bog.

'The ponies will never know what's hit 'em!' Gilda laughed. 'This might be one of my greatest pranks yet!'

Trixie joined in. 'And once the unlucky ponies who get a cup of 'juice' from this barrel take a sip, I'll swoop in and perform a magnificent spell to save them from the horrible taste!' she cackled.

'Personally, I think it's funnier not to save them ... but whatever you want, Trix!' Gilda said. The two of them high-fived.

'Hey!' Twilight shouted. 'You two!'

Gilda and Trixie scrambled to cover up the barrel, stepping in front of it to create a shield. They looked around but didn't see anyone until Twilight climbed out from behind the bush. A couple of twigs were still stuck in her mane.

'What are you, the undercover juice police?' Gilda sneered. 'Do you take all your orders from Applejack now? Or are you finally giving some orders of your own, like a real royal pony, eh?'

Twilight was a little bit offended. 'Well,

if you *must* know, I couldn't care less
what you do with that apple juice,' she
said, even though she knew she would
definitely tell Granny Smith which
barrel was filled with slime later. 'But …
I wanted to ask you about…' she couldn't
seem to find the words to ask Gilda
for help.

Trixie tapped her hoof on the grass
impatiently. She was still wearing her
purple magician's robe and pointy hat
covered in stars. 'The Great and Powerful
Trixie doesn't have all day, Twilight!' She
was clearly still a little bitter about the
time Twilight accidentally revealed her to
be a fraud in front of all of Ponyville.
Trixie probably didn't feel so 'Great and
Powerful' after that.

'What were you talking about the
other night at my cottage?' Twilight

asked Gilda.

The griffon shrugged casually. 'I was just saying that if *I* were a princess, no one would be allowed to tell *me* what to do.' Gilda put her claw on Twilight's shoulder and dug in a little too sharply. 'What is it that *you* want to do, Twilight?'

'I want to...' Twilight hesitated. It felt strange to be asking for Gilda's opinion on the matter. But she *was* right. Why was she spending time and energy listening to her friends, when she herself knew exactly where to find the answers – the one place she always felt completely at ease, no matter where in Equestria she was? 'I want to go to the library! The Crystal Empire Library!'

Gilda nodded in satisfaction. 'I'll admit – the library thing is a little weird. But the Crystal Empire sounds awesome!

You know what's best, Princess Twilight!'

A moment later, Twilight's jewelled necklace began to cloud and darken even more. Twilight didn't notice.

But there was definitely a new determination in her eyes. And it was a little scary.

All that Twilight could think about now was that huge library in the Crystal Empire. It held hundreds of old books! There was no way the spell wasn't hidden in the pages of one of them.

'Thanks for your help,' Twilight told Gilda and Trixie. 'I have to go to the Crystal

Empire now!' She spread her wings and took off into the air.

'That sounds so totally awesome! I'm coming, too,' Gilda said, flying alongside her. 'Is everything really made of crystals? What are the ponies like there?' Gilda began to imagine all the innocent victims whom she could play her pranks on.

'Trixie will go with you, too!' Trixie exclaimed. She pictured a whole new city of ponies who had never seen her 'Great and Powerful' magic act.

Gilda and Trixie followed as Twilight soared through the air, winding through Ponyville and unaware of everything in her path. Fluttershy, who was leading a line of baby ducklings back to their mother at the pond, noticed Twilight approaching. 'Hi, Twilight!' she said. She smiled and waved. 'I'm so glad you're here! I came up with some new ideas for the baby-animal sanctuary that I wanted to share with you...'

But Twilight didn't even see. Fluttershy's pretty pink mane blew out from the gust of wind Twilight's wings created. Rarity watched in pure shock. Who was this pony and what had she done with their best friend, Twilight Sparkle? Twilight always stopped to talk to her friends. Then Rarity noticed that the Cosmic Spectrum gem on Twilight's necklace had lost some of its shine. This was a bad sign.

'Oh, Fluttershy!' Rarity said, trotting up to her. She was carrying a large sketchbook in her pack. It was full of new outfit designs she had been drawing for Twilight's imaginary kingdom. Even though she'd been annoyed after the meeting, she still wanted to help.

'Do you think she heard me?' Fluttershy squeaked sadly. 'Twilight would never ignore someone like that on purpose, would she?'

But before Rarity could mention the necklace, Gilda the Griffon called out to them.

'Twilight is a princess now, you guys! She's off to the Crystal Empire and doesn't need a bunch of silly Ponyville friends like you. She told me so herself. ' Then she took off into the sky after Twilight.

Rarity and Fluttershy exchanged a worried look. 'We'd better go and find Spike,' Rarity said, looking to the sky. 'He'll know what to do.'

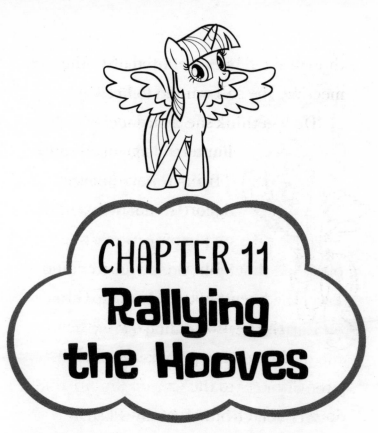

CHAPTER 11
Rallying the Hooves

The lights were on inside Golden Oak Library, but Rarity and Fluttershy had knocked on the door three times and got no answer. 'Is anyone at home?' Fluttershy whispered.

Rarity scoffed. 'You're never going to get his attention like that! Watch and

learn, darling.' She cleared her throat. 'Spiiiiike! Are you theeeeere?' Rarity trilled.

Spike flung open the door. 'Hi, Rarity!'

Fluttershy wasn't offended that Spike hadn't greeted her. Everyone knew Spike had a major crush on Rarity. He was holding a large tub of ice cream and looked like he'd been crying.

'Are you OK?' Fluttershy asked.

'Twilight left me behind again!' Spike wailed. 'She went back to the Crystal Empire and didn't even tell me! I had to hear it from Cranky Doodle Donkey.

'Unfortunately, it's true,' Rarity said, entering the cottage. 'We saw her leave.'

'No goodbye or anything,' added

Fluttershy. 'Just whoosh! And gone.'

'I think we can all agree that Twilight has not been herself today,' Rarity said. 'And I think that necklace is to blame!'

'Huh?' Spike and Fluttershy were confused.

'Last night I was trying to explain that although Cosmic Spectrum is beautiful, it can be dangerous if it is exposed to too many negative feelings. It absorbs them and makes the pony wearing it feel worse!'

'Poor Twilight,' said Fluttershy.

'I knew it wasn't her fault!' Spike said. 'We have to go and save Twilight. Together?'

'Together!' shouted Rarity and Fluttershy. Now all they had to do was find their friends and explain to them what had happened.

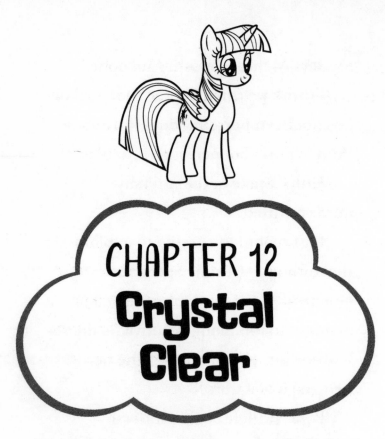

CHAPTER 12
Crystal Clear

'Look, I don't care what you do,' Twilight snapped at Gilda and Trixie. 'Just don't make any trouble!'

Twilight was almost at the Crystal Empire Library when she ran into Shining Armor. 'Twily? I thought you were in Ponyville!'

'I was, but now I'm back again!' Twilight said, shifting from hoof to hoof anxiously. She was itching to look through those books.

'You must have lunch with me and Cadance in the castle,' Shining Armor said.

'That's sounds nice, but I don't have time – maybe tomorrow. Talk to you later!' Twilight said, cantering past him.

He watched in confusion as she ran off. Normally, she was excited to see him. It was odd behaviour, especially for Twilight...

Shining Armor took off towards the castle. He had to find his wife, and fast!

★ ✦ ★

It was a familiar scene for Twilight, sitting in an accidental fort made up of large, glittery books. She hungrily flipped through the pages of one called *Ancient Spells of the Crystal Empire: Volume Four.* The Crystal Heart Spell just had to be in there somewhere!

'Twilight! Are you in here?' Princess Cadance called out. Shining Armor had come to her after seeing his sister act so oddly. Something wasn't right, and he knew Cadance could help.

'Yes, I'm in here,' Twilight sighed loudly from inside her book fort. She didn't want to see Cadance right now.

'Oh dear, Twilight…' Cadance shook her head. 'It's just as I suspected.'

'What is?' Twilight whined. 'Me being as big a failure as I am? A pony with no leadership skills whatsoever?' Twilight hung her head in defeat.

'No, no, no. You're not a failure,' Cadance said. She pointed her hoof at Twilight's neck. The Cosmic Spectrum wasn't shining at all any more. 'Look! You've got so down on yourself and others that the necklace is magnifying your negative feelings!'

The young princess looked down at the gem, stunned. 'I didn't even notice that it had changed.' Twilight thought of all her friends back in Ponyville. Rarity had tried to warn her about the gemstone, but Twilight had been so distracted trying to find the spell that she hadn't listened.

Actually, Twilight had dismissed all of their ideas. She thought of Pinkie Pie's cake day, Applejack's family dinner time, Rainbow Dash's Pegasus royal guard,

Fluttershy's baby-animal sanctuary, and Rarity's kingdom fashions. The ideas didn't seem so bad now. Her friends were only trying to help. And how did she thank them? By ignoring them.

'Oh, Cadance, I've been so horrible to my friends!' Twilight said, standing up. Several nearby books toppled over like a set of building blocks. The necklace began to glow dimly. 'I have to find them right now and apologise!'

Princess Cadance watched her gallop out of the library. Twilight was on the right track again.

CHAPTER 13
PFF to the Rescue

'Where do you think she'll be?' Applejack said as the five ponies and their baby-dragon companion made their way through the gates of the Crystal Empire. The last time they'd all visited was during the Crystal Faire. Everything looked just as pretty and shiny as it had before.

Rarity sighed. 'Why am I not a Crystal pony?' she said, remembering how her coat had become temporarily  glittery when they'd recovered the Crystal Heart. Unfortunately, the effects had worn off.

'What's that?!' said Pinkie Pie, pointing to a large crowd of Crystal ponies gathered near the fountain. 'Whatever it is, it looks like fun! I'm gonna go see!'

All of a sudden, a bright flash of white illuminated the sky. *Pop!* A loud noise rang out. 'Come on, everyone!' Applejack shouted, leading the way.

Applejack shoved her way to the front. A red-and-white-striped tent was set up.

Posters hung on the sides, praising the talents of **THE GREAT AND POWERFUL TRIXIE, MAGICIAN EXTRAORDINAIRE.** Gilda the Griffon stood outside the tent. 'Step right up, Crystal ponies!' Gilda shouted. 'Get yer tickets now! Step right up to see Equestria's most talented Unicorn –
the Great and
Powerful Trixie!
Only three bits each!'

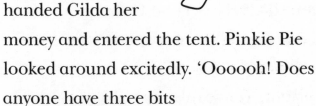

A yellow pony
with a golden mane
handed Gilda her
money and entered the tent. Pinkie Pie looked around excitedly. 'Oooooh! Does anyone have three bits
I can borrow?!'

'Don't they know it's a scam?' Rainbow Dash said in disbelief.

Gilda continued on, unaware that the Ponyville crew was standing in the crowd. 'Trixie is so powerful that she once defeated an ursa major – all by herself!'

A couple more Crystal ponies paid Gilda and entered the tent.

'Hey, that's not true!' said Fluttershy. 'It was Twilight who did that. Well, she took care of an ursa minor, anyway.'

'I can't stand by and watch this any more,' Applejack said. She trotted to the front and hopped up onto another crate. 'Crystal ponies! Do not pay to see this show! This griffon and Unicorn are con-ponies who are trying to steal your bits!'

A low murmur broke out through the crowd.

'What are you doing here?!' Gilda spread her wings and screeched. 'First you don't know how to take a hint when Princess Twilight wants to get rid of you! And now you are ruining our show?

Trixie peeked out of the tent to see what was going on. The Crystal ponies all watched the scene with their jaws open. This was more of a show than they'd bargained for!

'No one wants you guys here!' Gilda yelled.

'That's not true!' A voice pierced through the crowd and interrupted the argument. 'They are my best friends, and *I* want them here!' Twilight trotted over to her friends.

'What are you guys doing here?' Twilight asked.

'We came to rescue you, silly!' Pinkie Pie said matter-of-factly.

'I told them all about the necklace,'

Rarity explained. 'We knew
that you weren't being yourself.'

'The Twilight we know
would never be mean to
her friends!'
Fluttershy said.

'Or ditch
us for those
two!' Rainbow
Dash added,
motioning to
Gilda and Trixie.

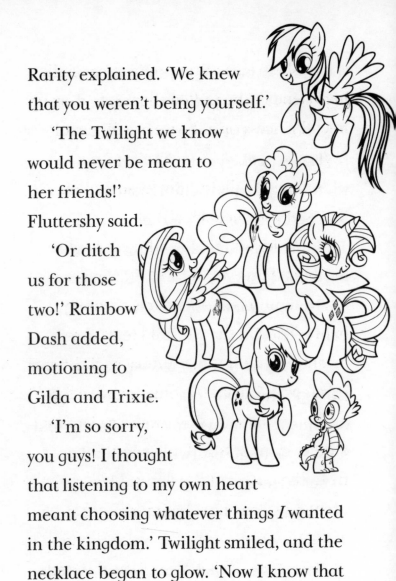

'I'm so sorry,
you guys! I thought
that listening to my own heart
meant choosing whatever things *I* wanted
in the kingdom.' Twilight smiled, and the
necklace began to glow. 'Now I know that
a princess is not defined by the things she
chooses for her kingdom. All that matters

is how she treats other ponies, especially
her friends.' She pulled them into a group
hug. 'Princess or not – we are all equal
ponies!'

'Oh my, Twilight!' Rarity squealed.
'Look at your necklace!'

Sure enough, the gem began to glow
brighter than ever before. The light was
low and pulsating, like a true beating
heart. Nearby, the Crystal Heart grew
brighter as well. It was almost as if the two
jewels were linked by some invisible force.
The ponies watched in awe as a gigantic,
glittery rainbow suddenly burst forth
from the centre of the Crystal Heart. It
arched directly into Twilight's necklace!

'Ooooooh...' all the ponies cooed.

'Hey, look at that!' Rainbow shouted.
'There are words on the Crystal Heart!'

Twilight knew it right away. The

Crystal Heart Spell had finally revealed itself to her. She trotted over and admired the words, which were lit up in shimmery gold. She took a deep breath and began to read them aloud:

'FRIENDSHIP IS THE CREED. IT HAS BEEN FROM THE START! IT'S THE ONLY WAY TO LEAD – WITH YOUR CRYSTAL HEART!'

Twilight's coat sparkled as the spell took its effect on her. *Of course!* she thought as she read the words. Friendship had always been the answer to her problems. Why did she think it would be any different once she became a princess? Twilight looked around at the crowd of Crystal ponies cheering her on, her best friends standing next to her, and her brother and Cadance looking proud.

Twilight finally felt like a real princess.

'Happy Cake Day, everyone!' Pinkie Pie shouted with glee, skipping through the centre of Ponyville. Since returning from the Crystal Empire, Twilight had started using all of her friends' suggestions as practice for being a real leader someday. Everywhere Princess Twilight looked, pony families were enjoying Crystal berry cupcakes and pies together. 'Happy Cake Day!' they said to one another happily.

The Cutie Mark Crusaders had even

made a banner that read PONYVILLE CAKE DAY! and hung it across the front of the town hall. 'Great idea, Princess Twilight!' Mr Cake shouted from the treat cart. 'These things are selling like hotcakes!'

'They are hotcakes, dear,' Mrs Cake laughed.

'Don't thank me!' Twilight said, walking over to where her friends sat on the grass. 'Thank Pinkie Pie! She has the best ideas!'

Twilight took a bite of her cupcake, careful not to let her tiara fall off her head. Wearing it still took some getting used to, but everyone really liked it when she did. 'In fact, *all* my friends have the best ideas.'

Rarity smiled and winked at her. 'So do you, *Princess* Twilight. So do you!'

Read on for a sneak peek of the next exciting MY LITTLE PONY adventure,

Rainbow Dash and the Double Dare

It was almost midnight in Ponyville, but nopony was tucked into bed yet. They all had the same good reason for staying up past their bedtime: there were only four minutes to go until it was *time*. Time for the most epic adventure ever to be released – *Daring Do and the Volcano of Destiny*!

'Omigosh, omigosh, omigosh!' said Rainbow Dash, a blue Pegasus pony with a rainbow-coloured mane. She began to pace around the patch of grass outside the Ponyville bookshop. Even though she would have the book in her hooves in less time than it took for her friend Pinkie Pie to throw together a party (her current record is four minutes, seventeen seconds), Rainbow Dash still felt so fizzy with anticipation that she thought she might explode. As awesome as a rainbow firework would look, however, she didn't have time for it. Not on the release night of the most incredible adventure book *ever*! Plus, if she exploded, she'd lose her place in line.

Three more minutes, she thought. Hardly any time at all! Yet it seemed like an eternity.

'Can't you ponies hurry it up in there?!' Rainbow whined as she peered through the bookshop window. The light was on and there was some movement inside, but the CLOSED sign had not been flipped around to OPEN just yet. Giant posters of Daring Do adorned the shop windows. They showed the famous adventurer Pegasus wearing her signature outfit – a khaki helmet and an olive green shirt. On the new book cover she was shown standing at a volcano bubbling with fiery red lava. The words above bore the book's title: *Daring Do and the Volcano of Destiny.* Below the cover, the poster read **MIDNIGHT RELEASE PARTY! GET YOUR COPY BEFORE EVERYPONY ELSE!**

Rainbow glanced at the large crowd behind her. It looked like two hundred ponies were there. Thank Celestia, she was first in line! Nopony else loved Daring Do as much as Rainbow Dash did. To prove it, she'd been camping out since the morning. She had brought all of the Daring Do books with her and had spent the day rereading them. When midnight struck, she wouldn't have to wait a single tick of the clock longer to find out what happened to Daring next.

The Daring Do series of books had become extremely popular lately, and Rainbow Dash suspected it was mostly because of her. She was a major trend-setter in Ponyville. Other ponies looked to her for anything awesome. So it was only natural that the bookshop had decided to make it a special event. Some of the ponies in line wore Daring Do costumes, and some munched on goodies from Applejack's treat cart. But they all had one thing in common – they were beyond excited to continue reading about Daring Do and her thrilling adventures.

'Get yer Apple Fritters...of Destiny!' Applejack said, trotting up and down the line with a tray of treats for sale. 'Fresh Caramel Apples... of Doom!'

'Hey, Applejack?' Rainbow asked her friend. They just

looked like normal treats to her. 'Uh…
what are you doing?'

'Figured I'd try to make my treats
sound as Daring Do as I could,' Applejack
explained. She passed a mini apple pie to
Rainbow. 'Apple Pie of Fate?'

'Thanks, but no,' Rainbow said,
pushing the treat away. 'It's almost time!'

Plot Twist, the yellow Earth pony with
an orange mane who owned the
bookshop, poked her head out of the
door to count the ponies in line. 'So
many readers!' she observed with delight.

'We're almost ready, everypony!' Plot
Twist shouted. She was glad she had
recruited Pinkie Pie to help her with the
party. They had expected a large crowd,
but nothing like this.

'Oh, man!' Rainbow squirmed. 'This is
taking forever!'

'Hiya, Rainbow Dash!' Pinkie Pie chirped, poking her fuchsia mane out of the window. 'Are you, like, so totally excited that you feel like you're going to  burst into a rainbow firework of happiness now that you're going to get the new Daring Do book first?!'

'Exactly!' Rainbow nodded. 'Now, can we get this show on the road? I have a story to read! I have to know what happens with Dr Caballeron! Is the Volcano of Destiny his secret lair? Or is it a decoy to distract Daring from finding the Secret Stables of Crickhowell?' With each word, Rainbow inched closer to Pinkie's face like she was interrogating her.

Pinkie shrugged and smiled wide. 'I don't know, but it won't be long before you do! We're just putting the finishing touches to the replica of Ahuizotl's temple we made. It's built completely from books! Isn't that totally readeriffic?!'

'Yeah, yeah. Very cool. But hurry it up!' Rainbow said, jogging in place. She'd been outside for a long time. Her legs and wings were starting to cramp up. And since she'd been waiting alone, she hadn't had one chance for a flying break.

Rainbow had tried to get her friends to come, but none of them had wanted to wait all day long. Fluttershy and Rarity had stopped to visit but had to go and tend to some newborn goats and finish sewing hats for them. Twilight Sparkle loved Daring Do, too, but she had decided to wait until her copy arrived in the post the next morning. She mumbled some nonsense about needing sleep.

It was so silly! What could be more important than this?!

'Only one minute left, everypony!' Rainbow Dash shouted to the line. Her call was met with cheers. The sound of the crowd triggered something inside of her. It was more than enough time to make a grand entrance into the

bookshop! If she flew at the door at just the right angle ... yeah, she could do this. She would do it for Daring Do!

Rainbow Dash turned to Applejack's

big brother, Big McIntosh, who was behind her. He was wearing a Daring Do helmet and chewing on a piece of hay. She'd have to trust him to keep her place. 'Watch my spot, Big Mac!' she shouted.

'Eeeyup,' he said, nodding his light orange mane.

'Hey, Daring Do fans! Watch *THIS*!' Rainbow hollered. The ponies all started chattering. What crazy thing was Rainbow Dash going to do now? The store was about to open!

Rainbow bolted into the air, beating

her blue wings as hard as she could. She shot off, a rainbow trailing behind her

that was so bright it was visible in the
night sky. If a pony had blinked they
would have missed it.

'Hey, where'd she go?' asked Apple

Bloom, pointing to the sky.

'There she is!' squeaked Sweetie Belle.
'She's headed straight for the door!'

Up in the sky, Rainbow Dash could see
the sign on the door flip from CLOSED to
OPEN. The door was still closed, but if
she'd calculated the timing correctly,
everything would work out perfectly.
She'd be the first to get the book and
she'd do it with style.

'Here I coooooome!' Rainbow shouted

as she completed a perfect triple barrel roll across the sky, leaving a corkscrew rainbow in her wake. Rainbow Dash swooped down. Everypony in line held their breath. Would she crash into the door? Apple Bloom and Sweetie Belle shielded their eyes with their hooves.

The ponies gasped as Rainbow hurtled forward, about to make contact. Then, at the very last second, the door opened!

'Iiiiincomiiiiiiing!' Rainbow yelled as she dived through, narrowly missing Plot Twist, who had come to greet the fans.

Bang! Boom! Crash!

All that was left of the grand towering

replica of Ahuizotl's temple was a big pile of books with a rainbow Pegasus in the middle. Even though Rainbow's stunt had ruined the display, it was a good thing the books had been there to soften the landing. At least that's what Rainbow told herself as she looked around at the destruction. Sometimes it took a little sacrifice to do something impressive, so the trade-off was worth it.

Read Rainbow Dash and the Double Dare to find out what happens next!

Dear pony pal,

Here are some super
exciting bonus pages
just for you.
Why not share them
with your friends too?

Love, Twilight Sparkle

Twilight Sparkle's Magical Mystery

What do you remember from Twilight Sparkle's exciting story? Try this quick-fire quiz.

1 **Where do Princess Cadance and Shining Armor live?**

a) Crystal Empire ☐　　b) Crystal Kingdom ☐　　c) Crystal Mountain ☐

2 **Which evil enchantress did Princess Cadance defeat?**

a) Pyramid ☐　　b) Pristine ☐　　c) Prismia ☐

3 **Who suggests 'Cake Day' as a new official Ponyville holiday?**

a) Rarity ☐　　b) Pinkie Pie ☐　　c) Applejack ☐

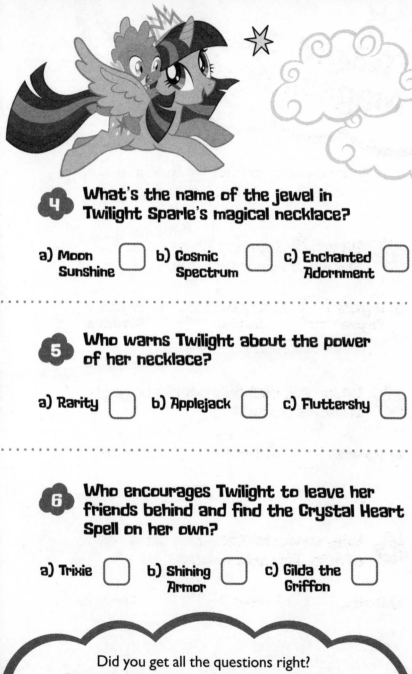

4 What's the name of the jewel in Twilight Sparle's magical necklace?

a) Moon Sunshine ☐   b) Cosmic Spectrum ☐   c) Enchanted Adornment ☐

5 Who warns Twilight about the power of her necklace?

a) Rarity ☐   b) Applejack ☐   c) Fluttershy ☐

6 Who encourages Twilight to leave her friends behind and find the Crystal Heart Spell on her own?

a) Trixie ☐   b) Shining Armor ☐   c) Gilda the Griffon ☐

Did you get all the questions right?
Check the answers at the bottom of the page.

Pony Profile

Here's everything you need to know about Twilight Sparkle!

Species: Alicorn

Element of Harmony: Magic

Cutie Mark: A star

Likes: Reading about magic

Dislikes: Surprises

Pet: Owlowiscious

Twilight Sparkle Dots

Join the dots to complete this picture of Twilight Sparkle. When you've finished, why not colour it in too!

Fit for a Princess

Twilight Sparkle is now part of Equestrian royalty, but do you know where she and the other princesses live? Match the pony to their home by drawing a line between them.

TWILIGHT SPARKLE

PRINCESS LUNA

PRINCESS CELESTIA

PRINCESS CADANCE

CANTERLOT CASTLE

CRYSTAL CASTLE

GOLDEN OAK LIBRARY

Did you get all the questions right? Check the answers at the bottom of the page.

Lost in the Library!

Twilight is busy reading every book she can get her hooves on to learn how to be a princess. Now Spike is lost somewhere in all the books. Can you help Twilight find him?

Crystal Empire Wordsearch

Twilight is learning about the Crystal Heart Spell. Can you help her by finding all the magical words in this wordsearch? Words can be forwards, backwards or diagonally.

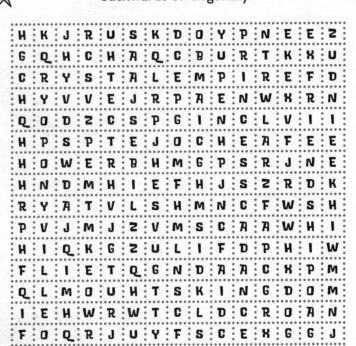

H	K	J	R	U	S	K	D	O	Y	P	N	E	E	Z
G	Q	H	C	H	A	Q	C	B	U	R	T	K	X	U
C	R	Y	S	T	A	L	E	M	P	I	R	E	F	D
H	Y	V	V	E	J	R	P	A	E	N	W	X	R	N
Q	O	D	Z	C	S	P	G	I	N	C	L	V	I	I
H	P	S	P	T	E	J	O	C	H	E	A	F	E	E
H	O	W	E	R	B	H	M	G	P	S	R	J	N	E
H	N	D	M	H	I	E	F	H	J	S	Z	R	D	K
R	Y	A	T	V	L	S	H	M	N	C	F	W	S	H
P	V	J	M	J	Z	V	M	S	C	A	A	W	H	I
H	I	Q	K	G	Z	U	L	I	F	D	P	H	I	W
F	L	I	E	T	Q	G	N	D	A	A	C	X	P	M
Q	L	M	O	U	H	T	S	K	I	N	G	D	O	M
I	E	H	W	R	W	T	C	L	D	C	R	O	A	N
F	O	Q	R	J	U	Y	F	S	C	E	X	G	G	J

CRYSTAL EMPIRE
PRISMIA
PRINCESS CADANCE
KINGDOM
GEM
PONYVILLE
FRIENDSHIP

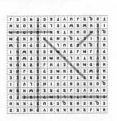

Answer:

Secret Spell

Is your spell:
- silly
- helpful
- exciting

Add these magical words:
- sparkle
- element
- special
- shimmer

Twilight uses her Alicorn magic to make spells come to life. If you could create a spell, what would it be for? Write it down below, using this guide to help you.

Name of spell: ....

....

....

....

....

....

....

....

....

What's Your Pony Name?

Find out your pony name with this handy guide. Why not work out your friends' pony names too!

Take the first letter of your name:

A - STRAWBERRY

B - DAREDEVIL

C - RAINBOW

D - STARBURST

E - VIOLET

F - SUNSET

G - TULIP

H - REBEL

I - LUNA

J - POPPY

K - RUBY

L - FIRE

M - PEACH

N - FIERCE

O - HAPPY

P - SUNSHINE

Q - BUTTERCUP

R - DISCO

S - DANDELION

T - FUZZY

U - FLASH

V - TWINKLE

W - GIDDY

X - DAYDREAM

Y - BUBBLE

Z - PRANCING

And the month you were born:

January	– MOON
February	– MANE
March	– FLASH
April	– BLOSSOM
May	– SPRINKLES
June	– TAIL
July	– PHOENIX
August	– WINGS
September	– CLOUD
October	– BEAM
November	– SNOWFLAKE
December	– GLITTER

My pony name is:

....

Your Pony

Species:

Cutie Mark:

Likes:

Dislikes:

Pet:

Now you know your pony name, it's time to create your very own pony character. Decorate and colour in the pony on the page, and fill in your own pony profile. Are you a Pegasus, a Unicorn or even an Alicorn? It's up to you!

Triple Twilight

Can you find the picture of Twilight that's different from the others?

Did you get the question right?
Check the answer at the bottom of the page.

Fun with Friends

Twilight Sparkle loves to spend time with her friends. Here are some ideas for things you can do with yours.

Write your own short story together!

You'll need at least one friend. Simply get a blank piece of paper and start writing the first sentence. When you've finished, pass it on to a friend and when they've finished they pass it back to you or to another friend. Soon you'll have written your own Daring Do mystery!

Throw your very own tea party!

You'll need some friends to come over. Oh, and some tea and cakes too!

Friends fashion show!

Why not model your favourite outfits with your friends? Maybe you and your best pals can swap fashion tips too!

Nature Trail!

Next time you're outside with your friends, why not jot down what plants, birds and animals you spot. You'll notice nature is everywhere!

Journey to Ponyville

It's time for Twilight Sparkle to get back to her home in Ponyville. But only one of these paths lead there. Can you show her the way?

A

C **B**

Did you get the question right?
Check the answers at the bottom of the page.

Congratulations on completing all these extra special puzzle pages. Twilight and Spike are off to read more about magic!

See you soon!

Discover more magical MY LITTLE PONY books!

OUT NOW

OUT NOW

EGMONT